BROKEN AGAIN

By SHARI COCHRAN

Published by Comet Publishing
U.S.A.
www.burtonprinting.com

Printed by Dave Kinder
Burton Printing Company/Comet Publishing
4270 S. Saginaw St.
Burton, MI 48529
(810) 742-3210
email: burtonprinting@gmail.com
www.burtonprinting.com

ISBN: 979-8-9912631-0-8

Foreword

Mom, be woman enough and admit that you never loved me. Dad, you could not have either lying to me. Like this is my heart, you all are messing with. Trust if I attained the lesson from the beginning, there would be no end. I got the message now between suppressing my emotions through self-inflection and harassment caused by depression. My presence became questioned because of Satan's omnipresence surrounding me. It steered me to understand that only God knew. Does anyone not understand what life after death is? None of you do. How can one pretend to be my parent while being dishonest? Both of you lied about Dad's death with the understanding of how much he meant to me. Then you both dare to confront me as if I am the problem.

Does anyone recognize the emptiness within me? Why should I give you the best of me? Mom, you took everything from me. You called me a mistake! What mother wishes death upon her children? Do you not understand the pain behind those words at twelve? Do you not care what it did to my self-esteem? It shattered and damaged me. I felt psychologically defeated. Do you not fathom the hatred I have for myself? Mother, you took away my innocence before I could enjoy life. Now, I shield my heart daily from pain, so I have zero to gain. People violated me in more ways than one. Foolishly, all those broken promises men gave to me when they raped me left me clueless and useless.

Sometimes, as a child, I used to stare in the mirror and hate the woman staring back. The woman on the other side of the mirror was invisible but thought she was invincible. Losing my ride-or-die almost killed me. Without Dad, there is no reason to be around. I ask God, "Why was Mom not killed instead of Dad?" With no answer, I slit my wrists to feel numb, not to think of the outcome. God, you took everything and everyone who matters to me away. I cannot trust anything you or anyone says. I lost everything. I'm never going to heal from wounds that shaped me. Yes, Heavenly is the problem. Around the clock, I felt humanity reminded me how weak and misunderstood I am. For many nights, days, seconds, and hours, I prayed for anybody or somebody to love me. My family couldn't communicate love. So now I'm convinced my heart has to become paralyzed and feel nothing. Mom, you pretend to be concerned about me. Asking, "What made me cold-hearted?" My response is, "You made a monster out of me!"

Dedication

This book is for my younger and present self. My life was/is far from a fairy tale but a failure. Society made me weak and broken to the point of no return. My crown has tilted left and right. Never; staying on but always falling off for people unworthy of my attention. No one can write my story but me. Rejection became my motivation. God, are you listening to me? Because it doesn't seem you are. For 30 years, I pleaded with God, but you were nowhere in sight! How could you allow the universe to decide my fate early on? Countless times, I wanted back inside my mother's womb. To escape the pain of reality. My peers chastised me. It ached so much I went to church for my preacher to baptize me. Life gave me PTSD. It sometimes appeared caged in pain, living in vain. Men, friends, and family neglected to recognize me. Outsiders playing tug of war with my emotions felt like a bullet to the chest. I am not bulletproof. Do you know how much heartache I had as a child? Nothing about me screamed extraordinary because I hated myself. Mentally, psychologically, and physically, the world persecuted me. Growing up thinking I was worthless. Nowadays, I'm second-guessing my life choices, criticizing my appearance, and eating to desensitize myself from actuality. I self-sabotaged because no one ever wanted me!

Why would anyone desire me when I don't? The Bible says, "No weapon formed against me shall prosper," but why are daggers relentlessly thrown at my heart? How can one not expect to go insane? Life has twists and turns no one sees coming. Mentally, I was bound to the past, unable to shake free from the shackles of imprisonment by my existence. I lost my mind trying to be something I'm not. If you look into my eyes, you will see someone barely surviving. My classmates didn't respect me at my best. So, I gave them my worst. At night, I lie in a fetal position, drowning in the anguish society inflicted on me. But can anyone rescue me from me? No. Daily fighting to stay alive.

My weight is constantly increasing and decreasing. Hair falling out left and right from the stress of life. I wasted seven years in school on a useless degree that didn't fulfill me. It sometimes felt like God abandoned me. Persistently, questioning the man above for my life is pointless. The Bible says, "If you have faith small as a mustard seed. You can move mountains". Where is it if you can't see it? God, I know you are there. Please, don't let life pass me by. I've allowed my dreams to fade into the wind in fear of failing.

It took me almost 32 years to understand the only person who had my back was God. Three years is how long it took to write this book because I didn't believe in myself. Not knowing the entire time, my biggest enemy was me. How was I supposed to know my identity when humanity chose it for me? Repeatedly, I listened to the voices inside, my head telling me I was powerless, afraid my peers would judge my work as mediocre. Hallucinating all eyes on me while writing this book almost took me out! I forgot I was a queen created by a king. When you level up, people aren't going to see you the same. It took me forever and a day to understand that Shari was not the problem. Shari, you are enough regardless of what anyone says or thinks of you. Allow me to reintroduce myself. My name is Shari Cochran. Be fearless, be strong, and be unapologetically you!

Special thanks:

This book could not exist if it weren't for the two important people in my life. Who inspired me to believe in myself when I could not. My inner demons overtook me for years, which is how long this book has been in limbo. If it weren't for my prayer warriors reminding me of God's gift, this book wouldn't prevail. Mental health is something unspoken of or ashamed of in the African-American community. I did not want to create a book for popularity but to bring awareness. Emotional/physical abuse, rape, mental health, and family neglect describe what this book is.

There are many instances where people remain silent and live in fear. Later on, you discover they committed suicide because they felt ignored. Therefore, I'm choosing my platform to be the voice for those who can't speak for themselves. Mom and Grandma, I love you both more than the words defined in the dictionary could describe. Life taught me to guard my heart at all costs. However, both of you made me understand God sees, forgives, and loves all. I promise long: as there is breath in my body, I will make you proud. Thank you. This book is for you.

Chapter 1:
SAME ROUTINE NOTHIN' CHANGING

My loyalty is to myself and my siblings. Mom, where were you at night when Chris or Ashley had nightmares? The person who was there wiping their tears or talking them off a ledge was me. There is not a day when we can count on you. We constantly make fools of ourselves to get noticed by you. What must I do to be seen by my mother? Every day, I blame myself for your abandonment. Never did I ever stop to think the problem was me.

Mom, you knew I was fragile from losing Dad. The sad part is you seemed not to care. The idea of losing the one person you could lean on and left to pick up the pieces became a lot. Emotionally, I became checked out. Life became intolerable to the point I considered suicide. The only thing that kept me from hanging myself was my siblings. My identity was vicariously in them. Without me, my siblings would have no one.

Every midnight, those are the thoughts and images shooting through my mind. Everything around me became questionable. I could not have faith in myself to be unaccompanied by my thoughts. All I did was rethink. Dad was my lifeline. Trying to be a role model to my siblings they could be proud of while missing dad was unbreathable. The only thing that keeps me steady is listening to Biggie Smalls Sky's The Limit. Every single time I hear it, it eases my nerves. Manifesting the life you require by craving a future even Satan cannot touch. It is marvelous. I desired loyalty, family, and freedom from drama. Listening to that song makes life seem possible.

Growing up in New York isn't for the weak. Occasionally, I get in my way. Trying to sleep is one of them. Tossing back and forth in bed in my thoughts causes chaos. It seems like an eternity. Curious to identify the time, I pivot to my nightstand to review the alarm that says 4 a.m. Angry is what I felt as time appeared to be at a standstill. No one comprehends the heartache I feel. Daily, I cry because I am stripped of my dad and left with a distant mother. Honestly, I question the man above. Praying every night is an illusion. Immediately, it regurgitates tears within me. I take a pillow, pull it over my head, and scream into it. Unaware that tears would benefit me, I stumble asleep out of nowhere.

Eventually, I nodded off until I overheard someone shout my name. Heavenly, come here. I jumped out of bed rapidly as if the apartment was on fire. To discover my sister Ashley freaking out because of a spider in her room. I said, "Ashley, relax. I will kill the spider. Please do not screech if you are drowning because it scared me." Ashley mentioned, "I did not mean to frighten you." Later, she sobbed as if I intended to punch her. I stated, "Misunderstandings will arise. Pick up from them and carry on."

While I killed the spider, I looked over at the clock that read 6 a.m. I motioned to Ashley and Chris, "Wake up, It's late. Both of you need to shower and get dressed in 30 minutes", I reiterated. This morning was unlike any other morning. Despite our differences, I went around the apartment looking for Mom. "Mom, I need money for lunch?" I yelled while searching for her. To my surprise, she is in the living room smoking. "Why should I give you money?" said Mom. I explained, "Now is not the time for an argument." "Here, take the money and go," Mom said, rolling her eyes. I walked away from her with my skin crawling in anger.

It is pathetic that I have to do her job as a parent. I am 16 and taking care of young children. But all she cares about is herself and drugs. All I could think what was wrong with her? I went into my room to pick out clothes for school. Just as I was about to go into the bathroom, there was a loud bang at the front door. I screamed, "Chris, get away from the door and get ready for school!" "Aw man, I can't do anything," said Chris. "What did you say," I asked. He said zilch but kept walking towards his room.

Afraid someone was trying to break in, I ran into the kitchen and grabbed a knife. Ready for whatever, I check through the peephole to see who it is. To my dismay, standing at the front door is our creepy neighbor, Tyrone. I closed the peephole and scratched my head, wondering what he wanted. Uncomfortable, I remained inside. "Mom is not here. Neither should you be," I hesitated. Instead of repeating that out loud, my response is, "Mom is unavailable, but I will tell her you stopped by." He responded, "Well, as soon as your mother gets home, tell her to pop up on me." Immediately, I began thinking, "That is not all you two will do." So, the only word I could get out of my mouth to reply to him was alright. All I could do was close the door and laugh.

A few weeks ago, as I was taking out the trash, I caught Tyrone and my mother through the window in his apartment in a romantic entanglement. When I saw Tyrone and my mother between the sheets, I couldn't help but puke. I ran back to the apartment to get the image out of my mind. Unfortunately, it was still there. Now, whenever he comes around, all I see is Tyrone naked. I have so many questions. First off, how does my mother, a nursing assistant, afford this place? But her personal life is her business. Despite my inability to understand, I could not bring myself to ask anything.

All I heard was dead silence. Apprehensive about whether Tyrone was still there. I gaze out the window. To my surprise, he left. I breathed an enormous sigh of relief. Tyrone can be intimidating. Walking back to my room, I reexamined Mom's entirety. Mom must have a double life. As I gather my things to shower, the clock says 6:30 a.m. I wasted 15 minutes talking to Tyrone about nonsense. None of us had showered or eaten anything. Immediately, I ran into the bathroom, brushed my teeth, and jumped into the shower for a few minutes to wash up. Hurrying to get dressed for school, I threw on anything. I'm always displeased with my appearance. Contrary to my depressive mindset, I decided to flip my hair into a ponytail.

With us running low on time, I checked in on Chris to see whether he was awake. To my disappointment, he was in bed, sleeping. Quickly, I did a double-take and slammed my hand against the wall to get Chris's attention. Yelling, "Chris, if you do not get out of this bed and shower in ten minutes, a spanking is waiting for you!" Chris leaped out of bed quickly, moving to the bathroom. Just as I was about to leave his room,

Chris ran to me with tears in his eyes. He asks, "What am I to bathe with?" I looked at him, puzzled, and realized it was time to go.

Ultimately, I left. As I stroll down the hallway to Ashley's room, Chris chases after me, hyperventilating. He was shaking because it stunned him to be alone. As I struggle to calm him down, I repeat, "I would never leave you home alone." Trying to reduce his shakes, I suggest we do some deep breathing exercises together. While we are wrapping up, I advise him to take a shower. Not to mention, after helping him, I have to check on Ashley. On my way to her room, I saw the door locked. I am baffled why.

Since we have no secrets in this apartment, I pound on the door. However, Ashley neglects me. I hollered at the top of my lungs. "What are you doing, Ashley... open this door?" Ashley replies, "Who is there?" Instantly, I became flabbergasted. Therefore, my frustration seeped, "You prefer to banter with me when we are behind on time." Unlock this door now! I hear her scouring off the bed, attempting to free the door. She unlocks it and asks, "How may I help you, sis?" I walked into her room, looking around to see what she was doing. Ashley was busy taking selfies.

Swiftly, I spun around and gazed at Ashley in disbelief. Instead, I explained, "I just wanted to see if you were ready for school. It looks like you are wonderful. Meet me in the kitchen so we can leave together. Let's leave on time," I clarify, leaving. Before I did, Ashley tugged at my arm. "What do you think of my selfie stick?" asked Ashley. Observing the device, I did not understand it. "Sorry, never heard of it. What does it do?" I inquired. She replies, "It collects pictures of me wherever I go at any length." My reply was, "Alright, perfect. Let's link up in the kitchen to take a selfie leaving the apartment." I fled.

On my way to the kitchen, I glance at my watch. It reads 6:50 a.m. Time flew by quickly. I began screeching, "Come on, it is time to go!! If neither of you is here in one minute. You'll be left behind and miss school." Instantly, I ran to my room to grab my coat, backpack, and shoes to head out the door. When I arrived in the kitchen, Chris and Ashley were dressed and ready to go. That put a smile on my face. Hopefully, we can make it to the bus stop on time; that is all I could imagine.

The bus will arrive in 15 minutes, meaning there is not enough time to eat. Considering our lateness, "I suggest you both eat breakfast at school since we are short on time." After putting on Chris's coat, we walk out the front door. While locking the door, I peeked at my watch. It says 7:00 a.m. I realize we are running behind. So, I grasp Chris's hand and gesture to Ashley, "We have only 10 minutes until the bus arrives. Move quickly."

While running, I noticed the bus lights flashing. Quickly, I pray, "Please, God, don't let us miss the bus." I look down at my phone; it reads 7:05 a.m., understanding we would not make it on time. As we are standing at the stop sign waiting for the cars to drive by, I see a street named "Martin Luther King." Immediately, I screamed to my siblings, "We're almost there." After mentioning that, I realized the bus was still a few feet away. Racing behind time to make it to the bus, I started wheezing heavily. Automatically, thinking we might be late, I notice Ashley is ahead of us. Immediately, I yelled, "Keep going, and try to get the bus to wait." Ashley said, "I got it."

Because of exhaustion, Chris and I began walking instead of running. My sister Ashley positioned herself in the middle of the street. As a crossing guard waving down the bus to stop. The driver put the bus in the park. Ashley motioned for us to come over to the bus. My brother and I began walking toward the bus. The driver allowed my sister to stand in the doorway while we loaded the bus, guiding us to our seats. Suddenly, the bus driver stopped and told me, "Tell your sister to stand back, or she can get hit by an automobile." My response to him was, "I would not let her do it again, but thanks for stopping the bus."

As we are walking to our seats, Chris sits next to me. He lays his head on my shoulder. Chris explained to me that he was getting out of school early. Today is a half-day. Mortified by the lack of warning, I had to assure him he wouldn't be home alone while not missing band practice and my math test. Therefore, I said, "My promise has always been I got your back. Don't worry. I'll be home when you get home from school. Just focus on being a kid and studying in class." Without a second thought, I hoped to keep that promise. In times like these, I wish we had a family. Being in two places at the same time seems impossible. I'm unsure how to accomplish this task. My school attendance is already horrible.

Instantaneously, I pricked my brain for solutions. Before I could decide, the driver announced that Douglass Elementary had arrived. Douglass Elementary is the school both my siblings attend. Before they left the bus, Chris began whining about his shoes not being tied. As usual, I snapped out of my fantasy to tie his shoes so he would not be late. After finishing, I reiterated, "Wait for me at the bus stop. I do not want you walking home alone." while zipping his coat. He nodded yes to me while hugging me. Chris and Ashley gathered their things and left. They turned around and waved goodbye, just as I did.

Repeatedly, in my mind, I wished a miracle could bring my dad back to life. If he were here, things might not have been as dire. At 11, I lost my father to a robbery held at gunpoint. I remember going into the kitchen late at night for water five years ago when I saw a police officer standing at the door. Mom was crying hysterically. I recall asking her what was going on. She said your father had an encounter tonight. Unsure what that meant. I placed my cup on the table and said, "Is something wrong with Dad?" She explained, "Dad had died." Not wanting to hear anything, I replied, "Lies." I did not want to hear anymore. I ran to my bedroom, slammed the door, and cried the night away. The day I lost my best friend, my ride or die, my biggest supporter. Nothing has been the same.

All I do daily is bask in my pain and drown in it. No ideas came to mind as my brain felt overloaded. Every time my siblings have an appointment or no school, I pay the price. Creating excuses is difficult now that Chris is getting out early. I suddenly saw a lightbulb inside of my head. Maybe there is a way I can explain to my music instructor that I have no one at home to watch Chris when he gets out of school. Hopefully, she believes me. Or I am leaving early. Ms. Wilson, my music instructor, is easygoing. Honestly, I want to quit playing the clarinet. Nothing about music brings me joy. Dad used to play the guitar in his spare time. I joined the band to feel closer to him.

Truthfully, I do not want to be at school today since I am the laughingstock of foolishness. Rumors and lies spread throughout the entire school about me. There is no one to confide in about anything. How am I to relieve stress? Looking into my surroundings to make sure no one is paying any attention. I reach into my pocket for a razor. Abruptly, I carve into my skin. It resulted in my eyes watering. I put my hand over my mouth to keep from screaming.

Chapter 2:
EVERYONE IS AGAINST ME

The bus finally arrived at my school, Malcolm X High. After I got off the bus, I walked toward the school. I felt alone, not wanting to embrace the day. I walked to my locker, and everyone was staring at me. Therefore, my trying to remain invisible could not happen. In the meantime, my heartbeat increased fast as I stowed away my backpack and jacket. All I could hear surrounding me were people gossiping or giving me funny looks. I repeated, "Heavenly, you got this. Don't let these people knock you off your crown".

As I gathered my books for class, I noticed Whitney down the hall. She is the most popular girl in school. Our friendship stretches back to kindergarten. Whitney and I used to be best friends. However, the glimpse of her walking toward me was like seeing a volcano soon erupt. Things have changed. Ever since her ex-boyfriend, quarterback Bryan, and I went on a date. Bryan spread rumors about us hooking up and how easy I was. Since then, the entire school has referred to me by numerous names. In reality, it couldn't be further from the truth.

Whitney was standing there as I finished collecting my books. We bumped into each other, causing them to fall. She began laughing and her minions. All I could do was not let her see me sweat. I assembled my things quickly. After standing up, Whitney catapulted me against the lockers. In the hall, a person replied, "Fight, fight." Instantly, there was a crowd surrounding us. Everyone was clapping and cheering on Whitney. Scared for my life, I respond to Whitney, "I apologize for anything you think might've happened between Bryan and me."

Whitney just sized me up and down. Rather than have faith in my answer, she commands, "If I ever catch you in my way or look at me funny, I will make it my business to see you don't make it to senior year." I nodded my head and ran away. My mind was racing a million miles per hour. Did Whitney threaten me? Am I weak? How did I allow her to talk about me like a dog in front of people? The answer is yes. I am confused about everything in life. But now is not the time to think about that because it's time to go to class before the bell rings.

Walking into English class, I take my seat. I weigh my options on how to be available for Chris. My school does not get out until 2:20 p.m., and Chris does not get out until 11:30 a.m. As a result, there is nothing I can do. My only option was to forego the rest of my classes for the day and band practice. Some days, it just felt like the world was against me.

Sitting at my desk, I daydreamed until my teacher called on me. He asked, "Ms. Brave. What year did the march on Washington happen?" said Mr. Williams. Unbeknownst to the question, I look out the window, contemplating how to block out the surrounding noises. Mr. Williams slammed a book on my desk to get my attention. The entire class began laughing. I apologized, "Mr. Williams, I don't know what the question was." Instead of giving a response, he walked away as the students in class laughed.

There is never a day where I am not the joke of something. I did what always worked and kept problems to myself. Time went by, and now I'm in the 3rd period. Math class is my favorite. Ms. Reed is the best teacher I've ever had. At the beginning of this semester, I struggled badly in math. Ms. Reed took me under her wing by setting up private tutoring sessions between lunch and the free period. Waiting at my desk for the teacher, I went over my study guide. I practically needed 100% to pass. As I continue to study, it becomes halted when Ms. Reed walks in.

Ms. Reed states, "Good Morning, Class. I hope you're ready for this exam. Remember, it's worth 50% of your grade. No pressure. Everyone, please do the best you can." I look at the clock, which reads 9:50 a.m. I have 1 hour to finish this test and leave to make it home on time for Chris. While taking the test immediately, I discovered none of these questions were on the study guide. Suddenly, I started panicking and overthinking that I would fail. Time was winding down with 30 minutes left. So, what I did next was unthinkable. I grabbed my books and backpack and ran out of the classroom.

While I ran out of the classroom, Ms. Reed yelled, "Heavenly, stop! Wait, where are you going? Get back here now." I turned to look at her with my eyes filled with water. Ms. Reed nor anyone else could comprehend my situation. All I did was scream before running off down the hallway. Stressing out about everything left me neglected and overwhelmed. Immediately, I made it to my locker, threw my textbooks, grabbed my jacket, and escaped.

Sadly, I am because Bryan stood at the front door. Surprised is an understatement to describe my feelings towards Bryan. Nothing about this day makes me want to continue living. This day is troubling as I struggle to collect my thoughts before having a nervous breakdown. Every fiber of my soul wanted to crawl under a rock and never emerge. Bryan looks at me, smirks, winks, and whispers, " No one will believe you." Seeing him with my own two eyes almost made me faint.

While I am sitting on the bench contemplating my life's choices, this mysterious woman walks over to me and says, "May I have a seat?" I nodded my head yes for her to take a seat. I closed my eyes to meditate but could not because of distraction. Even without opening my eyes, I could feel pain all over my body. The lady sitting next to me tapped me on the shoulder. She reached into her purse for some Kleenex and handed it to me. Instantly, after clenching it from her, I said: "Thank you." The woman explains, "Sweetie, you are in pain. Anyone with eyes can see that. Although we don't know each other, it aches me to see a young woman on a bench, ready to end it all. You tell me, how can I help?"

Right away, I broke out into tears. It was such a pleasure to be hugged by a stranger. I wrapped my arms around hers. No one has ever hugged me or asked about my feelings, not even the woman who birthed me. I pulled away from her and said, "I will be fine." The lady looked at me like she wanted to say more. Thankfully, the bus arrived. Before loading the bus, the lady handed me her card. She states, "Call me anytime you want." I ask, "Who are you?" She replies, "My name is Dr. Alexandria Williams."

Watching the woman leave, it felt like a ghost had just vanished. The lady was nowhere in sight as I searched for her before getting onto the bus as the driver blew his horn. This day was abnormal. Between people laughing at me, gossiping, skipping school early, and seeing Bryan, it almost caused me to run in the middle of the street and get hit. All of this seemed surreal. Therefore, it's becoming more challenging to stop replaying the day over. Then the bus announced, "Edison Way, this is your stop." Quickly walking off the bus, I found Chris standing, crying, tears flowing down his cheeks.

Instantly, I ran off the bus as the first one worried he would not be there. Chris saw me and ran fast. Without thinking, he hugged me, crying. Chris said, "I thought you had forgotten about me." I explained, "Now, why would I forget about you? You should know that I will go to the ends of the earth for you". He replied, "I know. But you terrified me by not being here." To reassure him, I was always by his side to snag his hand and walk together.

We finally made it to our apartment. As soon as I opened the door, propped up on the couch, to my revelation, was our mother, Shantell Brave. She asked us, "Why are you all home so early?" I said, "Do you want to know?" She then ignored me, continuing to smoke. Mom, you never care what we do, so why ask us now in front of strangers? No matter how invested Mom sounds, those were my opinions. Once again, Mom pays no attention to me, so I evacuate.

As I tried walking away, Chris nudged me on the shoulder. He reminded me of what Tyrone said earlier. My stomach filled with butterflies because I did not want to give this information to my mother. Stopping in my tracks, I angrily respond, "Mom, Tyrone came by earlier looking for you. He stated there was a problem to discuss with you." Instantaneously, Mom jumped up from the couch! She asked, " What did he want?" I decided not to answer and walked away. I chose not to answer and walked away.

Shantell Brave is the woman who gave life to me. Wholeheartedly, I never use the word, mom, because she is far from that. She was born and raised in Kingston, Jamaica. At eighteen, Mom moves to the United States for a better life. With no family or support, she worked two jobs to survive. Mom never really discussed her past. I always perceived if she talked about it, she would seem weak. It has always been us and no one else. No aunts, cousins, grandparents, or uncles around could help us. Even in our darkest times after Dad died, we fended for ourselves.

The only time I saw Mom show emotions or light up was around Dad. I remember her telling me how they met. Mom used to work as a housekeeper and server. One night at her job at Denny's, inside walks my Dad with some of his coworkers. Instantly, there was a connection between the two. Christopher Brave Sr. is my father. To me, Dad was a superhero. Everything I do is because of him. Dad worked as a construction worker, hoping to open his business someday.

Christopher Brave Sr. grew up in the foster care system. He never allowed his predicament to defy him. Anyone who knew my father knows he was an inspiration. It always brought a smile to his face whenever he aided anyone. My father would even give a stranger his last dollar. That was the thing my mother loved about him the most. His determination motivated her to become a nurse. As soon as my mother dared to apply for nursing school, she was pregnant with me.

Shocked by the news of the unplanned pregnancy, neither mom nor dad expected it. Immediately, they realized their dreams needed to wait. Both my parents came to a mutual agreement to get married. My parents honestly leveled each other out. Years go by as my parents bask in the afterglow of marriage. They became stagnant with their dreams. Enjoying the fondness for each other and being parents overshadowed anything else. Eventually, Mom decides now is the time for nursing school. Even my dad went after his aspirations, too. Unfortunately, life happened, and Mom was pregnant again. Time just never appeared to be on their side. No matter how hard they tried, they could not win. Instead of wanting a nursing career, my mother did not have it in her anymore for disappointment. Whereas my father kept faith that business would soon come.

For a while, there was no mention of anything. Since Mom and Dad were still working without interruptions, they planned a pregnancy. Nine months later, the baby arrived. Mom and Dad finally came to terms with their finished having kids. Each day, Dad continues praying for a miracle. One day at work, he gets promoted. Dad had the opportunity of a lifetime to be his boss. He was ecstatic and called Shantell with the splendid news. Mom was so happy for him that she even applied for nursing school. When it seemed everything aligned together, my father died. Every part of Mom died the moment Dad got killed. She forgoes nursing school and becomes a CNA. Mom eventually worked at Martin Luther King Hospital.

Rather than being a full-time mom, she became blind and in denial about not accepting Dad's death. Shantell started partying, drinking, smoking, and doing drugs. She left us for her friends and men. At 11, I became my siblings' mother. I have resented my mother ever since. Mom knows what buttons to push. She criticizes everything but does nothing. Instead of giving my mother a response, I ignored her and walked away. Before I did my homework, the voicemail machine light flashed. I checked the voicemail. Quickly, I noticed my school called with a message. With Chris standing beside me, I informed him," Go do your homework." Upon listening to the voicemail, "Hi, this is Malcolm X High calling to report Heavenly left school without permission. She's suspended until further notice."

Why does everyone have it out for me? Everything I do is for everyone but me. When is it time for something great to happen to me? Unbearable to think anymore, I ran into my bedroom to cry myself to sleep. While sleeping, my siblings came into my room to wake me up. Chris and Ashley jump up and down on my bed and scream, "We're hungry! Get up!" Forced to wake up, I stretch and wipe the crust out of my eyes.

As I walked into the kitchen to see what to cook, I decided on spaghetti. Ashley and Chris were both telling me about their day at school. My mother, who I thought had left hours ago with friends, was still in our apartment drinking. I told my siblings, "Finish eating because it's time to go to bed." Meanwhile, I went to tuck my younger siblings into bed. I explained to them, "I will stay up all night until mom's friends leave. Just go to sleep and not worry about anything". I headed back to my bedroom. As I leaped into bed, I turned on the TV to watch. Glancing over at the clock reads 2 a.m. I opened my door to see if anyone was still there. Everyone had left except my mother's boyfriend. Carlos is the name he lives with us.

Oblivious to his presence, I went back to my bedroom to sleep. Eventually, I fell asleep until I heard someone open my door. Instantly waking up, I realized it was Carlos. He locked my door and sat beside me on my bed. I pretended to be asleep. Carlos whispered with his hand over my mouth, "You are so fine, and I will have my way with you." "Stop! It isn't right", I sobbed as he continued to rape me. I tried to fight him off me. Instead, he pinned me down on the bed. I asked, "Please stop. I'm 16 years old." However, he didn't listen. He continued to have his way with me. Once he finished, he left my room.

Numb with what just happened, I began crying with the covers pulled over my head. I was still in disbelief at what had transpired. Instantaneously, I ran into the bathroom to take a shower. As I hopped into the shower with the water running over me, I crawled to the floor in tears. Thinking about what my life has become. All the pain, disappointment, and humiliation have driven me to hate myself. How can someone close as a father rape me? Everyone is playing these mind games as I can't or won't break.

However, I finished my shower and stared at my reflection in the mirror. Everything became raw. Immediately, I became angry and disgusted at what I saw. I believed everything people called me. For example, people saw me as: "easy, crazy, psychotic, and a mistake." Unfortunately, it became too much for me not to believe.

Instantaneously, I searched for scissors in the bathroom cabinets and drawers. After rummaging through the drawers, I found some scissors. I started chopping off my hair. Inch by inch until I didn't feel beautiful. Once I finished, I felt free from the bondage attached to my hair. My facial expression changed. Everything that was attached to my hair was how the world viewed me. My daddy used to call me "princess." Mom said, "I made a mistake." Here and now, I identify myself as a thought of blueprint but rather a misprint.

Tormented by what happened to me the night before, I slept at most one hour. This morning, my body felt nasty and distressed. I took out my journal to write a letter to my younger siblings, explaining how much I loved them. Regardless of what happens next, I needed them to know how much love and life they brought me. This thing called life has been too painful to live. I haven't grieved Dad's death. Lately, users and abusers have bombarded me. People pretend to love me to take advantage of my kindness. But I can't do life anymore without a dad. Therefore, I'm going to have to join him.

While expressing my feelings in a letter, I am interrupted by Ashley. She asks, "Lele, are you awake? We have to go to school, and the clock says 7:00 a.m". Unaware we were behind schedule, I grabbed her and jumped out of bed. After throwing on clothes, I yelled, "Let's go." Although we may not make it to the bus stop on time, I needed her to know zero was off-limits to discuss with me. I told Ashley, "In the event of anything or someone hurting you, you can always talk to me." She looked at me confused, asking, "Are you alright?" I forgot I cut my hair last night while Ashley gave me a look over. Not wanting to upset her, I nodded yes. Ashley replied, "I promise if I feel uncomfortable about something, I will talk to you about it." Relieved by this, we both walked into the kitchen.

Chapter 3:
SAYING NOTHING TO ANYONE

Rushing to gather their lunch together for school, I notice Chris is not in the kitchen. Instantly, I screamed, "Chris, get in here or stay behind! We are leaving in one minute". Abruptly, I handed Ashley her lunch bag. Chris was behind me, waiting for us. Ashley and Chris asked, "Can you check our homework?" I looked at my watch to see if we had enough time, but sadly not. Instead of answering them immediately, I moved us out the door.

Behind time, I locked the door. Chris and Ashley looked at me, disturbed. Chris asks, "Heavenly, are you alright? Why are you not going to school?" Ashley also nodded her head in agreement. My mouth dropped to the floor. There was nothing I could say to describe the loneliness and self-hatred. Instead, "I cut my hair because it was time for a change. Whereas school, I am suspended, but do not worry, it is not permanent". They just looked at me with no expression, their faces blank.

We finally made it to the bus stop. The clock reads 7:10 am no one is there. It scared me we were late. Simultaneously, just as I panic, a bus arrives. I sigh with relief as I watch my siblings board the bus. We both waved goodbye to one another. Because of this, I walked home. Once I arrived, I went to my bedroom, locked the door, and jumped back into bed. Not wanting to talk or think about yesterday, I developed no emotions toward anything. Rather than dwell on my problems, I slept.

Time flew by pretty quickly today. As I awoke from my sleep, it felt like an eternity. Out of nowhere, I received a text message from an unlikely source: my ex-friend Brittany. She and I used to be friends until Whitney got to her. Whitney convinced everyone I was desperate and psychotic. Tragically, because of this, Brittany only speaks to me when no one is around. Brittany's text states, "Hey, I wanted to check in to see how you are doing." My response was, "I am doing well." Brittany continues, "I am happy about that. Listen, I wanted to tell you about the rumors at school circling you had a mental breakdown earlier". Reading her response, I was unsure how to respond. Alternatively, I expressed, "Honestly, there is no truth to it." Brittany asked, "Can I drop by your house later so we can discuss it?" I explained, "Right now is not a good time. I am not up for seeing visitors". She answered, "Let me know when you can talk."

My encounter with Brittany through text messages was weird. I appreciated the text message alerting me to the rumors about me at school. However, I could not understand her. It's like we are cold one minute and hot the next. Brittany allowed outside forces to dictate her perception of me. So, I could not help but overthink this situation. How do I know if she is lying or not? Nothing is adding up. Regardless of the circumstances, I'm preparing to leave my house to get my siblings. Standing there waiting for me as I opened the door was Bryan. My heart sank completely inside my chest. Quickly, I tried closing the door on him; however, he pushed back. Bryan overpowered me, leading me to run to the back of my house. He continued chasing after me. Bryan yells, "Heavenly, can we talk?" Instantly, I ran into the bathroom and locked the door behind me.

Immediately, I started experiencing flashbacks of the night he raped me without my consent. No one knows I am pregnant by him. I started screeching, "Bryan, please leave me alone before I call 911. We have zero to discuss." Bryan did not like me threatening him because he pulverized the door. He yelled again, "Heavenly, open this door! I will not say it again". Afraid for my life, I dial 911. The 911 operator answered, "Are you alright?" Before I could respond, Bryan finally gave up arguing and went out the front door.

Out of thin air, I started crying. The phone in my hand fell to the floor. Every part of me froze. How is it that I feel unsafe in my home? Seeing Bryan bum-rushing me at home was breathtaking. My mind was racing too fast. It felt like experiencing birth. I scrambled up off the floor in search of a razor. Truthfully, I couldn't take this pain anymore. Therefore, I carved "ugly" into my left arm. No one ever called me beautiful.

The only word to describe how the world viewed me is "ugly."

Automatically, I take the chair in the bathroom and slam it against the mirror. Instantaneously, a million pieces shattered to the floor. My survival instincts set in. Life broke through me like I did this mirror. For me, it sunk in life was over. What am I going to do with a baby? I am only sixteen. Those men took advantage of me. All they perceived of me was an object rather than a person. The weight of our family struggles is on my shoulders. My siblings and I have no one to help. This environment is too toxic for anyone. I continued to slash my arms until I felt free. The floor had blood spattered everywhere, and I fell to my knees in a daze.

Unexpectedly, I passed out. While oblivious to time, I hear a loud thud at the door. Someone began yelling at the bathroom door, "Heavenly, are you in there? Seriously, answer us. Are you alright?" Wiping the tears from my eyes to prevent them from seeing how broken I am. To avoid confrontation, I explained: "Heavenly is fabulous but was taking care of business in the bathroom. Come here. Never be concerned about me disappearing. From the bottom of my heart, I'm sorry. Next time, Heavenly will be at the bus stop". Ashley responds, "It is alright, no worries. We just wanted to let you know we were home". As I hold on for dear life to avoid sobbing, I say, "Go do your homework now. I will check on you both later".

Instantly, I dropped my head between my legs. All this baggage from life keeps weighing me down. Why can nothing be right? It's like I am throwing my life away. Before I slipped back into my depression, I glanced at the clock. It said it was 5 p.m. Sadly, I was in the bathroom for an hour, sulking over misery. Nonetheless, of creating confusion with my siblings, I opened the bathroom door.

Sitting right beside the bathroom door was Chris, asleep on the floor. I sat next to him and tapped his shoulder. Chris jumped quickly and said, "What is wrong with you lately?" Although I wanted to divulge my issues with another person, I decided against it. On second thoughts, I answered,

"You have nothing to worry about. Let's go do your homework". I grabbed him by the hand while walking to his room. Chris noticed I ignored his question. He insisted, "Please don't leave us like Dad."

Wholeheartedly, I didn't know how to answer his question. Everything is already chaotic. All I could do was embrace him. Under no circumstances could I hide the truth from my siblings. I took the brunt of the beatings while covering my bruises. No wonder why every time they see me question everything. Predictably, Ashley and Chris could tell through my facial expressions the circumstances were exhausting. All I want for my siblings is to be kids and not worry. The option of enjoying childhood or being a mother was not for me. Regardless of their concerns, I will continue to put on a facade.

Following my conversation with Chris, I checked in on Ashley. Ashley was on her bed in her room doing homework. From my perspective, it looked difficult for her. Therefore, it led me to knock on her bedroom door. Ashley closed her math book. She said, "What did I do wrong now?" As I gazed at her on her bed. My reaction was, "Not anything. I wanted to see how school went. However, from your attitude, it appears terrible". Ashley became disappointed. She countered, "My grades in school are horrible. I cannot understand Math or English. Please help me". Ashley never complains. The idea of her becoming emotional informs me it's time to step in. Without hesitation, I state," I will tutor you. If I cannot comprehend, we will hire a tutor". She beamed and yelled," Thank you!" while squeezing me. After I finished embracing her, I left her room.

Meanwhile, in the kitchen, I prepare dinner. Everything about this day made little sense. The audacity of Bryan to show up at my place of residence uninvited was mind-boggling. After rapping me without permission, turning everyone at school against me makes me sick. Nothing about this was right. The one time I confided in Mom, she shut me down. I remember telling her that her boyfriend, Carlos, raped me. She screamed, "Why are you lying to me? Are you trying to sabotage my relationship with him?" I looked at her in disbelief because my mother did not believe me. I figured if anybody would understand trauma, my mother would.

Instead, she flatlined me emotionally. Immediately, I realized any words emerging from my mouth did not matter. Mom dismissed my feelings, causing self-doubt within me.

As I struggled to cook, the plate fell to the floor. Quickly assembling the pieces, fixing the dining table, and yelling, "Come eat." Immediately after I screamed, we gathered around the table to eat. Mom walks through the front door, ignoring everyone. Chris and Ashley look at me and whisper, "Is it alright for us to speak?" I nodded yes. Ashley and Chris screech, "Hello, Mom, how are you?" Mom did not respond but went to the refrigerator to grab some alcohol. Her not acknowledging their existence made me angry. Angrily yell, "Mom, Chris, and Ashley spoke to you. The least you could do is respond". She looked at me and walked away silently.

Astonished is the best word to describe her response. My mother went back to giving us the cold shoulder. I stared at my siblings crying and mentioned, "We are going to a hotel tonight. Grab your things and meet me in my room, packed in 30 minutes". I could not believe my mother. You ditch us for men. All you do is party your life away with your substance abuse friends rather than be a mother. The moment your children want to have a conversation with you, you become upset. We did not ask to be born; you had us.

Our living situation is toxic. I constantly felt imprisoned as a stranger in our home. There was regular impulsive reprimanded, overlooked, and abused. Emotionally drained, I went into the bathroom, grabbed the razor, and cut myself to feel better. Penetrating the blood out of my arm made me feel free. Truthfully, I felt as high as an airplane. Rapidly, I cleaned up the bathroom with no evidence left behind. Walking into my bedroom, I rummaged through my dresser for my secret stash. I found a pair of socks where I kept my getaway fund. While I counted the money, I noticed some were missing. There used to be 900 dollars in this drawer. How is it now that 200 dollars are left?

All I could think to myself was, "Why?" The men who sexually abused me walked free. Carelessly, I took money from them to get away. All I wanted to do with that money was escape. This prison called Life drove my money away. Does anyone like having their identity stolen from them? Well, I do not. I endured a lot to provide for my siblings. They do not know the pain inflicted on me by strangers. We do not even get any financial support from Mom. It is as if we are orphans staying in our apartment. So, if I have to recycle, babysit, or accept money from men abusing me. That is what I will do.

In my head, I kept over-analyzing how someone had stolen money from me. Nothing appeared to add up. Stressing from this caused me to burst into tears. How am I going to pay for a hotel tonight? I swear sometimes the man above doesn't hear me. Praying, crying, and indulging in self-harm don't help. Before I could dwell on my emotions, there was a knock at my bedroom door. Chris and Ashley yelled, "We are ready to go whenever you are." I expressed, "Alright, I will be out in one minute." Not trying to save myself, I went through my dresser to throw clothes in a bag so we could leave. Simultaneously, I asked my siblings, " Make sure both of you have everything needed, including things for school in the morning." They nodded yes, and we left.

While we walked out the front door, my phone rang. I noticed it was Bryan. How foul of him to think now is an appropriate time to call me? Walking to the bus stop, I had no idea where we were going that night. In my head, I kept thinking about what hotel or motel would allow a 16-year-old to get a room. Legally, you must be 18 to book a room. Which made me believe the only place that may help us is Motel 6. Finally, we approached the bus stop to wait to leave. This minute of enlightenment proved Mom cares for herself only. I realized Mom cares for herself only. After those shenanigans, she pulled earlier. Disowning we're her children; there's no coming back. Anytime I let my guard down with Mom, she always disappoints me by proving me right.

My heart breaks for my siblings, knowing I am all they have. It's times like these I wish Dad were around. He never made any of his children feel inferior or small. Right as we are about to take a seat, the bus arrives. While we loaded the bus, I paid the bus driver. Before taking a seat, I reiterated to the bus driver, "Please take us to Motel 6 on Cedar Avenue". As we sat, Chris said, "I'm going to take a nap. Let me know when we are there". All I did was laugh but reiterate, "As long as you are awake when we arrive." On the bus ride to the motel, I visualized life without Mom. Our mother should've been the one killed, not our father. Dad has been the driving force in motivating, pushing, and always dependable.

Finally, the driver said, "Alright, we've arrived. Cedar Avenue drop-off." Instantly, I slumped over and tapped both siblings on the shoulder in a deep sleep. However, they did not budge. I said, "Wake up before the bus drives off." However, they still didn't move. Hastily, becoming angry, I clapped my hands, screaming, "It's time to bounce off this bus." Immediately, they jumped up, and we walked off the bus. Walking down the street at 9:00 p.m. in New York is not something I would recommend to anyone. Eventually, about five minutes from walking, we see Motel 6, so we run inside. I told my siblings, "Let me do all the talking and not say anything that could jeopardize us getting a room. Inside, I see a male receptionist. He's beautiful, a youthful version of Chadwick Boseman. I believe he might be easy to convince.

Instantly, without reluctance, " Hi, my name is Heavenly Brave. I was hoping a handsome guy like yourself could help us get a room for tonight?" He goes, "I don't think so; you are too young." Shocked at his statement, I said, "I'm sorry. What did you say?" The young man sizes me up and down. He then says, "How old are you?" Seeing this stranger ask my age caused me to be angry. Instead of creating a scene, I answered, "Old enough to know asking me that question is redundant," I replied. I could tell he didn't like my answer because he stuttered. While scratching his head, he states, "Okay, well, I need to see some identification before you can get a room."

My brother Chris nudges my arm, yawning because he's sleepy. So, I pulled him in for a hug while searching for my ID. However, I couldn't find it. Instead, I looked at him, disappointed. "Unfortunately, I left my

ID at home. Please help us?" I ask. Before he could open his mouth, my sister Ashley chimed. "Listen, our mother works late. We are on the opposite side of town," said Ashley. I looked at her, astounded, shaking my head. The receptionist goes, "This is my problem. Why?" I ask, "Sir, what is your name?" He replied, "My name is Terrance." Immediately, I smile but snap back to reality. My response was, "Terrance, thanks for clarifying that for me. How old are you?" Terrance states, "I'm 18." My stomach soon filled up with butterflies inside, nervous about the outcome. My response was, "Great to know. But our mother is working until 3 am. We need a room." Terrance goes, "Alright. I will allow you to get a room this one time, but have your mother check in once she gets off work. OK, that brings your total for one night to 108.00".

Rapidly, I hunted through my purse for the money. The line behind us was long. As I counted the cash, it totaled out to 150.00. My hands shook as I handed Terrance the money. Terrance gave me back my change-plus room key. Deep down inside, I hoped we had enough money to make it home tomorrow. "Please take care of yourself," he said, looking at me concerned, handing me a receipt. In my eyes, you could see I was barely alive. My siblings and I took off to our room. As we make it to the room, I open the door. In anticipation of our vacation, I couldn't get in the room without Ashley and Chris pushing me out of the way. Instantly, they get excited, as if we hit the lottery. They dropped their bags to the floor and headed straight towards the bed to jump on it.

Truthfully, I have never seen them like this before. Our current living situation is insufferable for any human to endure. I allowed them to enjoy themselves until they fell asleep. While they bounced back and forth on the bed, I sat on the couch. In my head, I replayed the conversation with Mom. Shantell Brave and I have been going in circles for months. We've never been able to understand each other. Tonight, of all nights, Mom's disrespect became breathtaking. She reached new lows I didn't know were possible.

Sitting on the sofa with my hand on my head, I ran to the bathroom. Closing the door behind me, I cried in silence. I didn't want my siblings to suspect anything. Right now, Chris and Ashley are impressionable. They can take anything literally. I ran the sink water and snatched a towel before placing it on my forehead. My heart started beating fast. I couldn't help but think, was it panic or a heart attack? Immediately, I took a seat on the floor, breathing slowly. After counting backward from ten, I picked myself up to stand. I reached into my pocket to look at the receipt. Upon checking, I noticed Terrance wrote down his phone number. His audacity made me less interested. Terrance was the last thing on my mind. Therefore, I threw away the receipt. When I opened the bathroom door, Chris and Ashley were sleeping.

Grappling through my bag for pajamas, I glimpse over at my siblings awake. My siblings tricked me into thinking they were sleeping. "Alright, you two, it's bedtime. Since I thought you were already sleeping", I said. Instead of listening, they hopped up out of bed. Chris and Ashley tried to double-team me. They both yelled, "No sleep, no sleep." As I helped them into their pajamas, I screamed, "Yes, sleep!" Both of you have school in the morning." Ashley whined, "Do we have to go to school?"

Chris and Ashley stared at me with their big brown eyes glistening with water. I caved in. "Alright, I will let you both miss school tomorrow. If you can wake, bathe, dress, and be out at 6 a.m.." I explained. They smiled and said, "Yes, we will be ready." Chris and Ashley jumped into bed as I tucked them in. I kissed both of their foreheads and turned off the lamp.

Eventually, I put on my pajamas. Before going to sleep, I scanned my phone and noticed Mom and Bryan trying to reach me. Unfortunately, it wasn't a surprise. Neither one wanted a conversation meaningful to me until after we left. I ignored the calls and set my alarm for 4:30 a.m. We needed to be up and out before Terrance tried to expose us in the morning. I turned the lights out and went to sleep.

The very next morning, the alarm goes off at 4:30 a.m. Forcibly, I woke up and turned it off. I gathered myself, removed the blankets, looked at my phone, and saw several texts and missed calls from my mother and

Bryan. What a great way to start my morning off stressing over nonsense. Promptly, I'm reading through the text messages. However, one with my mom stands out. Mom implies, "I hate all of you. Never think of coming back home." Another text reads, "I miss your father so much I can't live like this anymore." Mom's text messages continued on and on. I didn't know what to think because she speaks gibberish when intoxicated. Then I read Bryan's message: "I know you might hate me, but let us talk. This is craziness, I miss you". Yeah, right, I thought.

Tossing my phone on the nightstand, I rose out of bed quickly. Wiping the crust from my eyes glance, at my siblings sleeping. I yelled, "Alright, you two, let's get up so we can shower and be out of here in 30 minutes." Struggling to get ready, I noticed the clock said 5:30. Rapidly, I pushed Ashley and Chris to clean as we were behind on time. Chris says, "I'm going as fast as I can." My skin crawled with anger. I ignored his response while packing. My answer is, "I know you're moving fast. But to not get caught being dishonest yesterday. We need to leave now." Ultimately, within a few minutes, we are making progress. Everyone was ready to go at 5:50. As I pushed Chris and Ashley out the door, we hurried to the bus stop. Quietly entering the lobby, I search for Terrance. Thankfully, he's nowhere in sight. We ran out of the front entrance.

Chapter 4:
WHERE TO GO FROM HERE?

Finally, we made it out of the motel without getting caught. As we stroll to the bus stop, I think about what type of home we are going to. Chris and Ashley depend on me for everything. If Mom disregards our feelings again, I am unsure what will happen. Out of thin air, I felt light-headed. Not equipped to deal with this, I pass out. Ashley and Chris turn around to help and ask, "If I am alright." Seeing their eyes tear up as they struggle to help me arise. My only option was to spare them the truth and lie. Instead, I explain, "Yes, please do not worry because I'm fine." I hugged and pushed them to keep walking.

While I watched my siblings walk off, I tried to stand up. Quickly, I placed both hands on my knees until they gave up on me. I almost fell until Terrance caught me. Terrance assisted me in getting up and asked, "Heavenly, is all well?" Utterly shocked by his appearance. I respond, "Where did you come from?" Terrance explains, "Well, I wanted to say goodbye earlier. Regrettably, I couldn't because you left. Alright, you found me, Terrance. What is so important? I asked with both hands on my hips. Terrance states, "I just wanted to know if you will go on a date with me?"

Frankly, I didn't know how to respond. Terrance asking me out is all I wanted. The idea of watching him become nervous as we approached the bus stop was sweet. We were practically standing near Chris and Ashley, who could hear anything. I reiterated, "Can I talk with you privately for a moment?" grabbing him by the hand. Immediately, I said, "Chris and Ashley, wait here for the bus." "Did I say something wrong?" asked Terrance, confused. My goal was to reassure him, "You said nothing wrong. I cannot go out on a date with you because of obligations". Terrance states, "Okay, I understand you're busy. But can we at least text?". Trying to think how to answer him, I respond, "Sure, we can text. However, I have to get back to my siblings before they worry." "Can I get a hug before you leave?" Terrance asked. "Certainly," I said while hugging him.

As I hugged him, I could tell it upset him. We waved goodbye to each other. I ran back over to my siblings as the bus arrived. We hopped on the bus and headed back home. During the bus ride, my uncertainty peaked at what just happened. The way I view it is out of sight, out of mind. There is no time to care for me. Instead, focus on what lies ahead for us at home. Walking through the front door, I noticed it was quiet. Mom was nowhere to be found, which was great. While placing my bags down, I see the light flashing on the answering machine.

Unfortunately, it was my school. "Hello, this is Malcolm X High. We are calling to discuss Heavenly's suspension. Please call us back as this matter is urgent." Why does my school need to speak with my mom? Did my secret become exposed? Is it about the rumors of me having a mental breakdown at school? All these opinions racing through my head had me nervous.

My siblings are the only reason for staying alive. I felt nauseous from overthinking every little thing. Life betrayed me in more ways than one. Nothing made me feel powerful but powerless. I ran into the bathroom to vomit. Not sure what I ate that made me feel sick. Leaving the bathroom, I went into Mom's room to see if she was still there. To my shock, she was not. All her belongings disappeared, and she left a note. Stating, "I cannot do this anymore as your mother. You are better off without me."

I did not know whether to be concerned or excited about this letter. Everything was already on my plate. But now I am worried about how long we can go on like this. With no family, friends, or money, CPS will find out. Out of nowhere, I started feeling this tightness in my chest. Unable to breathe, I tried shouting to my siblings for help. I clutched onto my neck with both hands for any sound but received emptiness. Instead, I crawled for a helping hand. Squirming on the floor for help in the hallway, I passed out.

Quietly, I awakened, and my surroundings detected cold and black. It felt like a nightmare. I searched around the house for my siblings to ask what was happening. But to my amazement, Dad is in the kitchen making them breakfast. Instantly, I knew this couldn't be real. I stared at him in disbelief. Dad looked at me like something was wrong. Immediately, I started crying. Dad stops cooking and hugs me. He wipes away my tears. Dad questions me, "Heavenly, what is wrong?" Everything in me couldn't plan a sentence. Instead, I became mute. Dad taps my shoulder. I lost balance and responded, "You do not know how many nights I prayed for your arms to hold me again. Father, please relieve me from this hole in my heart." Dad just continued to embrace. Rather than become skeptical, I sat and ate pancakes with the family.

Being okay with the uncomfortable is different. I want to be loved so badly that I'm willing to lose myself. Days, nights, minutes, and hours I crave/obsess with love. Sometimes, the new me wishes life had a rewind button to what reality could be. At the beginning of adolescence, there were no worries. My existence was innocent. Heavenly had her superhero dad to guard against the enemy.

I couldn't help but wonder if life was experiencing a time machine. Everything I prayed for these past five years was standing beside me. But How? Dad must be an angel sent to me by God because this can't be real. After breakfast, Dad walked Chris and Ashley to the bus stop. In the meantime, I stayed home basking in the irony of my father being here in the flesh. The moment Dad walks through the door from taking them to the bus stop, I will explain to him my pregnancy. No one knows I am pregnant but me. It will finally allow me to express, "I am pregnant!" without feeling judged. Right now, I am unsure what to do. Mom packed her bags and left. Meanwhile, I'm stuck with a mirage of Dad to lean on for guidance.

Waiting for Dad to return home, I ran around the apartment doing cartwheels. Despite Dad being gone a long time, I watched the clock and drifted off to sleep. Unexpectedly, as I was sleeping, someone pushed me to the ground. Incidentally, I jumped up, ready to fight whomever. Until I realized the stranger was Dad. Without thinking, I smacked myself several times to wake up. Simultaneously, blinking my eyes twice came, to an understanding that this was not a dream but reality.

Dad looked at me, puzzled. He motioned for me to join him on the sofa. Honestly, I didn't know how to react. Instead, I shook my head "no" and ran into my bedroom with the door locked behind me. I propped my head onto my pillow to cry. Immediately, I heard a knock at the door. Dad yells, "Heavenly, open this door. It's me. We need to talk." All I could interpret was a hallucination. "Dad, you're not here. As much as I wish this were true, it's an illusion", I screamed. No matter how much I missed Dad. One couldn't help but wonder if I was going crazy.

Meanwhile, trying to ignore Dad didn't help. He only grew angrier by the minute. Dad continued pounding loudly at my bedroom door. Nothing was working. Scrambling to escape, I attempted to pry open my bedroom window. Instantly, through the bedroom wall overheard, Dad kicked the door open with his foot. Coincidentally, I struggled to unlatch the window quickly. Then, out of nowhere, the window opened up. Immediately, I climbed out the window as Dad propelled and unbolted the door.

Chapter 5:
RUNNING OUT OF TIME

Ultimately, I made it outside. My adrenaline was on fire while running far from this place. Everywhere I turned was the image of Dad. In the background, Dad screams, "Heavenly, get back here!" I didn't care how frequently Dad called my name. There was no turning back for me. Eventually, I found myself five blocks from the apartment. Once I realized I could no longer hear Dad's voice. I fell to my knees. Everything in me broke out into tears.

Why do I keep lying to myself? Life can't be this cruel. Every time I try to do things right. Reality takes advantage of you. "Why have you forsaken me, God?" I yelled. I've never been to church in my life. However, I discovered this higher power from television. One night, while babysitting our neighbor's kids in the apartment complex. I saw a well-known bishop preaching on TV. His words from the television seeped into me.

Don't let what happens in this lifetime defy you. Yes, you may cry or become broken, but dry those tears. Please understand God hasn't forgotten you. What happens in this existence doesn't measure an eternity spent with God in heaven? All those nights of me praying, God would intervene when men violated me. My classmates, mom's boyfriend Carlos, and strangers who took my innocence before I could give it away were heart-wrenching. No one should ever feel cheated out of life. Where were you, God? When mom abandoned her responsibilities and left them to me? Nowhere. I had no choice but to begin life again and again.

My hands trembled, trying to wipe the tears from my eyes. How could my so-called family leave us? My anger boiled over. I've been a walking punching bag to people for over 16 years. In my head, I experienced flashbacks of betrayal from peers, men, and family. It's as if I'm losing control over everything in life. Mom walked out on us like it was nothing. Dad appeared out of nowhere like popcorn as a ghost. Now, my phone is blowing up with messages from Brittany and Dad.

Brittany's text states, "What's going on? Everyone at school is saying you snapped yesterday and left for no reason. I need an explanation of what's going on. Please, Heavenly, text me back. Know that I'm here for you!" Wow, that is all I could imagine. Brittany may not be my first choice for a friend. The reason is that she's always ghosting me in public but is my friend behind closed doors. Now, I need someone to confide in for guidance.

Immediately, I stood up with my energy and mind on one thing: revenge. Nonstop, I began running to Jefferson Street to catch the first bus. My first stop was to pick my siblings up from school. However, I couldn't leave yet. Instead, I continued waiting for the bus to arrive. Each second, it didn't appear my anxiety increased. The thought of everyone walking free from my abuse caused me to flip the bench over. Everyone at the bus stop looked at me, scared for their lives. All these strangers started backing up as if I were going to hurt them. Quickly, my voice screamed, "Yeah, I'm crazy." Enough of the criticism. No longer could my frustration be contained.

Thankfully, the bus arrived. Quickly, I bombarded everyone to be the first one on the bus. While I took my seat, all I could imagine was leaving this nightmare. Everyone broke me. I yelled at the bus driver, "Take me to Douglass Elementary now!" Ironically, I fantasized about what my journey would be like if I were dead. Let's be authentic. No one will miss me. Better yet, everyone's reality would be monumental.

My mind was racing a gazillion heartbeats away. I'm sick of hiding and pretending. To the world, I'm happy when it isn't true. Frantically hanging on for the bus to stop, my entire body quivered. On the ride, I continuously tried to talk myself off the ledge and remain calm by doing meditation practices. However, nothing worked until the driver yelled, "Douglass Elementary! Your stop."

Instantly, my mind snapped out of delusion into reality. Quickly, without hesitation, I tried to run off the bus. Out of nowhere, a stranger tugs my arm. He says, "Don't do what you're planning." There was nothing I could do but grab my arm back. Everyone had all eyes on me as an audience. Therefore, nothing was left for me to do but run off the bus and not look back.

Meantime the clock is ticking; we're running out of time. Freaking out, I open the school doors searching every classroom for Ashley and Chris. My mind is concerned for their well-being. Everything I did was unthinkable. My hands hammered every door, asking: "The teachers if they'd seen Ashley or Chris." All of them cooperated until one of the teachers called security on me. At this point, myself is livid. Frantically, I'm frantically whimpering my response, "Call the cops. Do what you have to do. But I'm not leaving here without Ashley or Chris!"

Things appear to be taking a turn for the worse. But what happens next is something even I didn't think through. In my right eye, I notice the security guard has a gun. Instantaneously absent-minded. I grabbed the gun and pointed it at everyone. One of the security officers asks, "Please remain calm. No one here has to get hurt. We'll find them for you." Each individual here is just like my absentee parents! No response from anyone. I decided to acknowledge, "No more stalling. Find them now or else." Everyone chose to ignore me. That caused me to scream again, "Ashley or Chris? It's me, Heavenly. Can you hear me?" Unexpectedly, a classroom door opens, and out goes Chris.

Chris walks toward me and stops. He glances at me with a gun and becomes frightened. My eyes immediately become filled with water. Never was it my intention to scare him. Before I could embrace him, he came toward me as Ashley. Without thinking, Ashley pleads, "Heavenly, what's going on? Why are you holding a gun?" Unsure how to respond, I hid the gun in my left hand. My ability to formulate a sentence was difficult. Therefore, I stammered, "Forget what you see going on here. Everything I do is for the two of you." Right when I turned my back, the officers snatched the gun.

Immediately, the officers threw me to the ground. Chris and Ashley try to stop them by kicking and screaming. Without thinking, I grabbed them with my arms. Chris and Ashley pulled me up as the officers were holding me back. Therefore, I must have the strength of Goliath because I stood with no problems. Rapidly, I took my siblings, and we left the building.

Chapter 6:
ALL OF IT CAME TO THIS

Exactly when we make it outside, I hear police sirens. My mind and heart palpitate 10 miles per second, afraid for our lives. Chris pulls my hand and insists, "What is that noise?" Casually, I hyperventilated about how long to keep up this charade. Chris and Ashley are already becoming suspicious. She replies, "Heavenly, what is going on? Are you having a mid-life crisis?" Not to make them more doubtful but reassuring. I cleared my throat and said, "Life is perfect. We are going on a field trip for a few days."

In addition, Chris and Ashley looked at me, disoriented for an answer to their uncertain future. Unsure how to reply, my head turned to the left and saw the police coming. Desperately striving to escape, I sign to them, "You will have the answers soon. Right now, we have to leave. Otherwise, the cops will separate us." Chris and Ashley nodded their heads agreeably. Therefore, we took off running. We ran until we could no longer hear the sirens. Running down Williamson Avenue, my leg hits the curb. Honestly, we did not make it far except maybe two blocks. My foot gets messed up pretty badly. It was intolerable to walk on it.

Hesitantly, struggling to move my foot, Ashley and Chris turn around to help me. Slowly, we walked up the hill as we saw no bystanders approaching. Next, I noticed a log for me to rest. My phone keeps ringing in my pocket. Struggling to get the phone, Ashley hands it to me. To my surprise, Terrance is calling. Why does he always text or call at the wrong time? Unfortunately, my mind was foggy. So, I texted, "Terrance, we can't talk now. My siblings and I are on the run and leaving. Have a nice life." After messaging him, he texted back immediately. However, there was no time to reply.

Finally, after all the struggles, my shoes came off with a piece of glass pushed deep inside my foot. The sight of my left foot was horrific. Neither Ashley nor Chris could stomach this. Instead, they ventured off into the forest to puke. My immune system is capable of anything. Lying on the ground, I reached into my jacket, grabbed a cloth, and used the other free hand to remove the glass. Nonetheless, I cried hysterically. Finally, struggling to clean up, my siblings returned, ready to go.

Ashley and Chris returned from their torturous adventure in the woods. They both asked if I was alright. God, I wish to be truthful but lied instantly with, "Yes!" We started back on our path somewhere, anywhere. Sadly, we had nowhere to go. No money, family, friends, or strangers to ask to allow us to stay with them. Frankly, the only viable option was to leave New York. I could not stomach returning home to the apartment to gather our belongings and see Dad. But it left us with no other choice.

People think karma isn't real, but God doesn't like ugly. Just because your heart is attractive doesn't mean it can't be unattractive. As we closely approached the street of our apartment, my stomach was on overtime with butterflies. Suffering from secondhand embarrassment caused me to become terrified walking into our apartment. The aftermath of last night created an unusual quietness.

My siblings and I sprinted into our bedrooms to gather our things to leave. Unfortunately, in my bedroom, a visitor was awaiting me. Instantly, I screamed, "Dad, what are you doing here? You're supposed to be dead!" Immediately, he closed my bedroom door and grabbed my arm. I yanked my arm away from him. Dad put his finger to his mouth and whispered, "Be quiet, heavenly. Because they'll hear you." Hastily, in disbelief pushed, away from Dad to cope with what was real or fake. My entire upbringing was a lie. Furthermore, I whispered to Dad, " How are you alive? I thought you were dead".

Something doesn't make sense. How are you dead one minute and alive the next? "Dad, I need answers! Nothing adds up. How can you leave us suffering in all this pain?"I hollered. There is no way I could look him in the eyes without dying. This entire situation has me disturbed. Recklessly, I propped the bedroom window open when Dad wasn't looking. In a no-win position, I rashly climbed out the window onto the fire escape skyrocketing ten stories.

Dad wasn't paying me attention because he searched the apartment up and down for me. All I could hear continuing to climb was Dad screaming for me. "Heavenly, where are you? I'm sorry for lying to you. Please come back or tell me where you are.", Dad yelled while panicking. However, it didn't work. It didn't matter how many times Dad shouted for me. There was no doubling back.

Eventually, I made it to the rooftop of our apartment in despair and tears. My hands covered my eyes, my chest was on fire, and hallucinations caused me to fall to the ground. Everything in my head felt like I was about to explode. I have been through trials and tribulations. How am I supposed to cope? God, everyone, is expecting me to fail? But I'm trusting in you to come through. This baby inside of me is an abomination.

Folks think I planned this. The answer is no. My virginity was the one thing I had control over! Nevertheless, l didn't. I'm a victim of rape which; is how this child came to be. Everyone is always taking something from me. God, somebody, please help me. I can't do this anymore. Those were illusions reoccurring of what society thought of me. Periodically, in my mind, I kept reverting to my siblings downstairs, subjected to this chaos. Out of nowhere, the rooftop door opens. There goes Dad, Ashley, Chris, Mom, and Carlos, walking as if nothing happened. They felt the need to ambush me without telling me! At that moment, all I saw was red. Instead of embracing them as they approached me, I ran off the roof.

Chapter 7:
DOES ANYONE KNOW WHAT THE TRUTH IS?

My eyes were closed as I fell from the rooftop into whatever destiny had in store. The moment my eyesight returned, death wasn't near. However, God had other plans, and he wasn't finished with me yet. All I could do was yell, "God, Why? Just kill me now, please. Nothing here brings me happiness." Being out of touch with reality, I hear Ashley and Chris crying in fear. Both are in tears, brawling: "Heavenly, are you okay? Please answer us. We cannot live without you". Although their responses were heart-warming, my heart couldn't stand living. At this second, I was tired of fighting and losing in life. Truthfully, there was no need for my siblings to see me disheveled. Therefore, my move was in silence.

Mysteriously, I morphed back into reality before landing. All I could do was scream for "help!" but to no avail. It was then I understood my fate. My home became unrecognizable. Nevertheless, it was time to end this toxic cycle by leaving. Sadly, only my feet could go in the direction of two blocks before collapsing in tears. Flashbacks in my head reminded me home isn't where the heart is. I'm tired of arguing with my supposed family. Right now, the struggle between reality and sanity is real. Nobody wants me! It feels like my emotions are getting the best of me. My phone has been blowing up with calls and texts.

Meanwhile, checking my phone, I noticed Terrance and Dad texted. Terrance is my only friend. My mind raced with imagination and adrenaline on a hundred. Despite being mentally impaired, I realized Terrance was probably the voice of reason. Maybe he will run away with me and help me figure out what to do with this baby. Even Brittany texted me," What happened to you? Why are your parents asking me if you are alive? Please tell me you didn't kill yourself. Call me now!" Shocked was an understatement to see she cared. But nothing is going to change my mind.

Every time, I wrestled with walking away. The universe brings me back to Martin Luther King Street. Is this a sign from God? New York isn't or hasn't been great to me. For the night to clear my psyche, I decided to rest in the alley. While sleeping, God and I had a confrontation. There were so many questions I needed him to answer. First, what's with all the secrets and lies? Or how about my dad lying about his death? How am I 16 to support a baby? What was the point of allowing men to violate me? All these were thoughts shouted in agony by me. Except, God's presence faded away into thin air. But before he left. God mentioned, " My child, I've never left you. The pain you're experiencing is fatal. I'm aware. But I died on the cross for my children not to endure as much torment as I did. Everything that has happened to you is for a reason. When you wake up, all will be communicated". In tears, I hollered, " What is going on? God, please don't abort me. I'm incapable of doing this life alone".

Nothing prepared me for what was to come next. The moment I woke up. Tired is the best emotion to describe me. Meanwhile, everything that happened to me the night before was a blur. My heart ached, and my head throbbed for no reason. One would think my family is concerned for my well-being. The answer is no. There were over 100 missed calls and text messages when I checked the phone. My family even went as far as putting an amber alert out for me. Coincidentally, it made me recall last night wasn't a dream but a fatality.

Is my "fake" family serious? All this has to be a joke. Quickly, I called Brittany, and without hesitation, she answered the phone. Brittany picked up the phone and said, " Heavenly, you're alive. Thank God! Do you know I've been up all night praying for you? I know we don't see eye to eye on everything. But don't try to off yourself because life has become insufferable!" At that moment on the phone, I was mortified and speechless. Why now does Brittany care? Instead of being combative or indulging in negative thinking, my response was more subtle. "Brittany, I'm touched by your generosity and concern. You've proven to me this time that you care. Does this mean I can come to your house to cool off?" I questioned. Nonetheless, Brittany didn't think twice. She said, "Come on over and stay as long as you need to."

Instantly, I gathered my belongings to head over to her house. Everyone keeps denying my pain. Am I not human? Before facing my family, time apart was what we needed. Nothing great could come from the multiple personalities I was experiencing. Everything in me wants to commit suicide again because this unhappiness is unacceptable. Regrettably, life isn't a time machine where I can change the past. New York felt unsafe. Walking to Brittany's house at 4 a.m. felt terrifying and exhilarating. But something in me couldn't shake the feeling someone was following. Earlier in the alley, as I collected my possessions, it felt like someone else was there. While sleeping for a few hours, it appeared a person was breathing over me. But I didn't think anything of it. Moreover, it seemed like a daydream turned into actuality.

Despite being nervous, I kept walking. Sporadically, I checked over my shoulders to make sure no one was following me. It wasn't until a sneeze caught my attention. Unhesitatingly, I turned around quickly and yelled, "If anyone is out there, show yourself!" Shockingly, to my avail, Bryan jumped out of the bushes and left me speechless. He couldn't say anything but tried kidnapping me before I ran away. Now, I'm praying for a miracle aiming to escape. Bryan screams, " Heavenly, you can't run. There's nowhere for you to go. Come here and face me like a woman. It's all over town; you are pregnant. You've been gossiping to everyone that I'm the father."

Frankly, I'm shocked to see Bryan this bent out of shape. All I could do was cry. "What's your purpose, Bryan? I'm sorry for everything. Please, don't do this. There's no going back only you know what you did to me", I explained while whimpering. But Bryan didn't want to hear my explanations. Instead, he gets angry and catches up to me. Quickly, he grabs me from behind. I tried with all my might to fight back, kicking and screaming. However, nothing worked. At this point, the survival course was a fact. All I could do was shout for help. The neighborhood we were in was predominantly white. Nobody heard me. My heart began beating fast. While struggling for my phone inside my pants pocket, I called Brittany. Brittany goes, "Heavenly, What's going on? Hello? Can you hear me?" Thankfully, Bryan didn't hear anything. Since Bryan's hand covered my mouth, I squealed to give codes to indicate Bryan had me. But to my dismay, Bryan used chloroform to make me unconscious. It was from there that everything went black.

Be on the lookout for my sequel book

"Invincible but not invisible"

Can you see me now? Do I have your attention? Well, what is it you all want from me? My baby! It is mine! Do I live rent-free in all your minds? Daddy, do you expect me to believe you're my father, or shall I say Christopher Brave? How could you do this to me when I idolized you? It seems like you and Mom have some explaining to do. I raised your two kids, my siblings' as if I were their parents. But you know they are mine and no one else's. You all think it's cool to pretend we are a loving family with each other, which is far from the truth. I'm tired of people misusing and abusing me. For almost 17 years, I was a figment of everyone's imagination. But now that I am pregnant, it's time to do me. Mom, miss me with your boyfriend Carlos, who raped me, by the way. He could potentially be my father. I told you once before what he did to me, and you chose him over me. I'm not a walking doormat.

Everyone at school caused me to have a mental breakdown. My only true friend, I pushed away because of my insecurities; Brittany can't even help me. Nonetheless, all these secrets and past traumas at home threw me into the hands of Bryan. He took advantage of my naiveness as a weakness. Now look at me kidnapped because of what everybody put me through! The truth is, I had no one for 16 years but myself! Even when chastised by my peers and so-called loved ones, God is who my faith was in. The Bible speaks of how God can see and hear your cry. All of them lonely nights sleeping on the streets, on floors, and in unhealthy environments. God was there. No one wants the truth to come out. Although the Bible says, "Death and life are in the power of the tongue," Maybe I cursed or jinxed myself for thinking negatively about everything! But no, it can't be because I'm the child, and you are supposed to be the adult in this equation! Folks believe my past wounds contribute to my becoming broken again. It may have, but to bring life to an unborn child brought strength like Samson had in the Bible. My life made me invincible so others would not see me invisible again!